Sebastian Explores

To Mum and Dad

ISBN: 978-1-935021-28-5

Library of Congress Control Number: 2008907924

This edition first published in the United States 2009
by Mathew Price Limited,
5013 Golden Circle, Denton TX 76208
Text and illustrations copyright © 1990 Vanessa Julian-Ottie
Cover Design by Empire Design Studio

Vanessa Julian-Ottie

Sebastian Explores

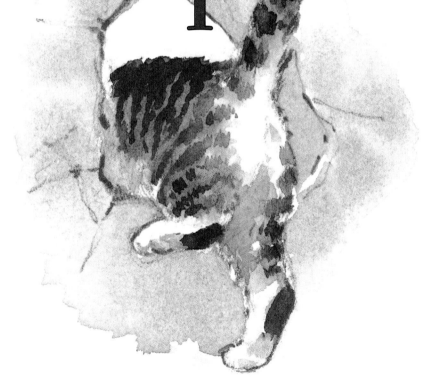

MATHEW PRICE

Sebastian was playing in the garden with his
brother and sisters when he saw a butterfly.
"Wait for me, butterfly!" he called.

He jumped through the wall and
landed on a pile of straw. Two little mice
ran away as fast as they could.

"Wait for me!" said Sebastian...

...and ran straight into the chickens.
"*Cluck, cluck, cluck,*" they squawked.

Sebastian stopped running when he came to a hole in the fence. Something was moving around on the other side.

In the field was a very large brown animal.
"*Meow*!" cried Sebastian.
"*Moo*!" said the cow.

The cow was friendly but Sebastian
didn't want to stop. He scampered through
a hole in the old stone wall.

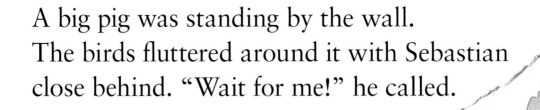

A big pig was standing by the wall.
The birds fluttered around it with Sebastian
close behind. "Wait for me!" he called.

Splosh! Mud flew everywhere.
It was time to head home.

Sebastian jumped over the wall.
"Oh, no!" he cried. "Look out!"

"*Eee-Aaw!*"
The donkey tossed Sebastian straight
through the window,

...straight onto the sofa. "Where have *you* been?" asked his sisters. "Just exploring," said Sebastian.